NO TIGHTS FOR GEORGE!

George has to wear tights in the school play and he's in a real twist about it!

June Crebbin was a primary school teacher before taking early retirement to concentrate on her writing. She is the author of a number of books for children, including *The Curse of the Skull*, *Emmelina and the Monster*, *Tarquin the Wonder Horse*, the picture books *Fly By Night*, *The Train Ride*, *Danny's Duck*, *Into the Castle* and *Cows in the Kitchen*, as well as several volumes of verse and three titles for beginner readers in Walker Books' Read Me series. A frequent visitor to primary schools, where she gives readings, talks and workshops, June Crebbin lives in Leicestershire with her husband and her rabbit.

Books by the same author

Carrie Climbs a Mountain

Emmelina and the Monster

Tarquin the Wonder Horse

For older readers

The Curse of the Skull

JUNE CREBBIN

No Tights for George!

Illustrations by Tony Ross

WALKER BOOKS
AND SUBSIDIARIES
LONDON • BOSTON • SYDNEY

For Michael and all his friends at
Churchtown Primary School

First published 2002 by
Walker Books Ltd, 87 Vauxhall Walk
London SE11 5HJ

2 4 6 8 10 9 7 5 3 1

Text © 2002 June Crebbin
Illustrations © 2002 Tony Ross

This book has been typeset in Garamond

Printed and bound in Great Britain by
The Guernsey Press Co. Ltd

British Library Cataloguing in Publication Data:
a catalogue record for this book
is available from the British Library

ISBN 0-7445-5999-5

Contents

Chapter One

George slammed his schoolbag
down on the kitchen table.

"I hate being in the school play!"
he exploded.

"But I thought you loved it," said
his mother. She frowned at him.

"I thought you wanted to be the green helper of the Green Wizard who lives in the green castle."

"Not," said George fiercely, "if I have to wear green tights!"

Mum fished inside his schoolbag and drew out a pair of tights.

"What's wrong with them?" she asked.

George took a deep breath. "I'm a boy," he stated. "Boys do not wear tights."

"Oh," said Mum. She looked at George carefully. "Who said?"

"No one," said George.

But someone had.

Slimy Barry Butcher, sliding round the edge of the hall when they'd been trying on their costumes.

"GIRLS wear tights!" he'd sneered at George.

George had turned away. But Barry Butcher grabbed his arm, twisting the skin between his hands until it burnt. George gasped with pain.

"GIRLIE!" hissed Barry Butcher.
George rubbed his arm. If only
he'd been chosen as the Green
Wizard, he thought. The Green
Wizard wore a long flowing robe.
No need for him to wear tights.

"Ballet dancers wear tights,"
Mum said.

George winced. "MUM! I AM
NOT WEARING—"

"Don't shout at me," said Mum.
"I'm not the one who's been saying
things. I'll sort it out in the
morning."

And sort it out she did, with the
whole of Class 1 straining to hear
every word.

It wasn't difficult. Mum and Mrs Bicks agreed, in VERY LOUD voices, that of course boys didn't wear tights nowadays, but in far-off days, in the long-ago days of the play, it was perfectly normal.

Over my dead body, thought George.

The tights would have to go.

Chapter Two

That afternoon, as soon as George arrived home from school, he rushed upstairs to look for the tights.

They weren't on his chair. Or on his bed. Or in the wardrobe.

"Where's my costume?" he demanded, tearing back to the kitchen.

"All washed and ironed," said Mum, folding the tights and the green tunic carefully. She popped them into a carrier bag and hung it on the door handle.

"Good," said George.

He sat down. All he had to do now was wait for the right moment. He tried not to look at the carrier bag.

"Mrs Bicks says you're really good at helping the Green Wizard with his spells," said Mum.

"Mmm," said George.

Mum picked up the pile of ironing and took it upstairs.

At once, George leapt to his feet, snatched the tights out of the bag, ran down the garden and stuffed them down, deep, deep down into the smelly bottom of the dustbin.

Then he jammed the lid back on as well as he could – it had never been a good fit – and flew back to the house.

Dustbin Day tomorrow.

He'd never see the tights again.

Chapter Three

George didn't hear the crash in the middle of the night as a fox tipped over the dustbin, scattering its contents all over the path...

When he woke up, he just felt happy. The tights had gone.

He went down to breakfast.

On the back of his chair hung a pair of very dirty, very smelly, but very definitely green, tights.

George flinched.

"Well?" said Mum. She waited.

"However could they have got like that?" said George.

"You tell me," said Mum.

George thought quickly.
Sometimes the truth was best.

"I threw them away," he said.

Mum sat down. "Go on."

"I TOLD YOU BEFORE!" shouted
George. "I DON'T WANT TO
WEAR THEM!"

Mum sighed. "Well, you can't
wear them today, that's for sure."

Later on, she had a quiet word with Mrs Bicks.

At playtime, Mrs Bicks had a quiet word with George. She said George must tell her AT ONCE if anyone was being unkind.

George said nothing.

At lunchtime, when he went to the toilets, people kept banging on the door and shouting: "Georgie Porgie, pudding and pie, wets his tights and starts to cry..."

"I'm not wearing tights!" shouted George. "I'm never wearing them!"

But he knew by the time he set off for school the next day, the tights would be washed and ready to wear.

He had to get rid of them properly. Once and for all.

So that they couldn't come back.

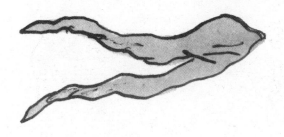

Chapter Four

George still hadn't thought of a
plan as he and Mum set off for
school the following morning.

"You're very quiet," said Mum.
George managed a smile.

They passed a letter-box.

That's it! thought George. *I could post them. I could just push them into a letter-box. Then they'd be gone.*

He remembered there was another letter-box by the school crossing. Mum always chatted to the lollipop lady. He'd do it then.

When they reached the crossing,
a crowd of people were waiting.
George was ready. As soon as
the lollipop lady spoke to Mum,
George turned the other way.

Quickly, he stuffed the carrier bag with the tights into the letter-box and just managed to catch up with the last few people crossing while the green man was still blinking.

Mum was waiting. "Where were you?" she asked crossly.

"I got caught in the crowd," said George.

George skipped down the last bit of road, past the last house where the friendly puppy chewed your gloves to bits if you let him.

"Have a good day!" said Mum at the school gates.

George smiled.

He marched into school.

The tights had gone.

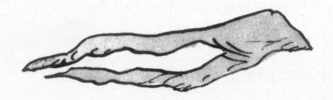

Chapter Five

It was a good day. Except when Mrs Bicks asked him where his tights were and people giggled. Still, he was able to reply truthfully.

"I don't know," he said.

They could be on their way to Peru, or China, or Manchester by now, he thought happily. Though he hadn't actually put them in a parcel, so they were probably in a dustbin somewhere. Probably at the Post Office. The postman would just throw them away.

"Had a good day?" said Mum,
when she met George out of school.

"Oh, yes," said George.

"How did the play go?" said Mum.

"Fine," said George.

That afternoon, as George's
mother was making the tea, there
was a loud knock at the front door.

"I'll get it!" said George.

George opened the door.

A cheery postman stood on the step. He pulled a pair of green tights out of a carrier bag.

"Thought you might be needing these, Robin Hood!" he said.

George gasped. "No thank you," he said. It was all he could think of. He stuck his hands behind his back to stop them taking the tights.

The postman stopped being cheery. "But they were in this carrier bag," he said, "with this envelope. There's a shopping list on the back but..." The postman turned it over and showed George the front. "This is your address," he said, jabbing the number with his finger.

George flinched.

"Who is it?" Mum called.

"I'll talk to your mother, shall I?" said the postman. "I haven't got all day. I've got my collections to do."

George snatched the tights from the postman's hands. "I've just remembered," he said. "They are mine. Thank you."

George shut the door. He pushed the tights up his jumper. Mum appeared in the hall.

"Who was it?" she asked.

"No one," said George.

"Well, it must have been someone," said Mum.

She opened the door.

George held his breath. He peered out from behind her. No one. Only the sound of a van pulling away.

"Could have been someone knocking and running away," said George helpfully.

"Mmm," said Mum. "Very odd."

George ran upstairs. He threw
himself on his bed and pulled out
the tights. Now what was he going
to do with them?

By morning, he had the perfect
answer. He couldn't think why he
hadn't thought of it before.

He skipped along beside Mum
all the way to school. Down the
long road, across the busy road
and down the last bit of road.
Then, he lagged behind. Mum
walked on ahead, chatting to her
best friend.

There, at the last house, was the friendly puppy leaping up and down at its gate, hoping for a wisp of glove or a snippet of scarf.

"It's your lucky day!" George whispered to the puppy. He pulled the tights out of his pocket and fed them through the bars of the gate.

The puppy seized them in his
teeth. He shook them and growled
at them. Then he settled down for
a good chew.

"George!" called Mum.

"Coming!" yelled George. He ran to catch up.

This time the tights had gone for good.

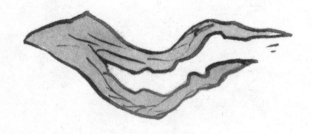

Chapter Six

It was just after playtime when
Mrs Bicks handed George his green
tights. She didn't ask questions.
She said she expected George must
have dropped them on the way
to school.

"Luckily, the caretaker rescued
them before that puppy down the
road chewed them to bits!" she said
cheerfully.

She dusted them down and dried
them and handed them back to
George when they practised the
play. There was nothing he could
do. He had to put them on.

"You look a right cissy!" hissed Barry Butcher. Lots of people giggled.

George put on his green tunic
and his tall, green pointed hat with
the big red L for Learner and tried
to concentrate on the play.

He loved helping the Green Wizard with his magic spells. He had to hold the Big Book of Spells up high so that the Wizard could see it. But he held it too high and no one could see the Wizard.

"We must get it right," said Mrs Bicks. "This is our last practice. Your parents will be here tomorrow."

At last she swept everyone back
to the classroom to get changed.

George picked up his trousers
from the pile of clothes on the
desk.

"They're mine!" said the boy next
to him, snatching them away. "See,
they've got my name in."

George looked through the pile again. There were no more trousers. He looked under the desk. He looked on the desks near by.

Everyone else was ready.

"Come on, George," said Mrs Bicks.

George went hot as everyone
turned to look at him.

"He can't find his trousers!" said
Barry Butcher.

Everyone laughed.

"Rubbish!" said Mrs Bicks. "We must all search. They must be here somewhere."

But the trousers were not there.

"I'm afraid you'll have to go home in your tights," said Mrs Bicks.

The class gasped. Some people laughed.

George stood there miserably.
Was there no end to his trouble
with tights?

The classroom door opened.
The headteacher came in, followed
by a man carrying a camera.

"This gentleman," said the headteacher, smiling at everyone, "wants to take a photo of you in your costumes to put in his newspaper."

There was a buzz of excitement.

"Oh dear," said Mrs Bicks. "I'm afraid we've all just got changed. It's the children's home-time."

But the man was beaming at George.

"Come on, Robin Hood, I'll have
you!" he said.

Everyone stared.

"Of course!" said Mrs Bicks.
"George is still in costume."

"But he's not Robin Hood," someone shouted. "He's the Wizard's helper!"

"Even better!" said the man, and whisked George away to the library with the Big Book of Spells.

The next day the play went well, George's trousers were found, and when his photograph appeared in the newspaper, Mrs Bicks pinned it up on the classroom wall. Everyone crowded round to see.

"You look great!" someone said.

"You look WIZARD!" said someone else.

And everyone laughed and agreed.

More **SPRINTERS** for you to enjoy!

- *Little Stupendo Flies High* Jon Blake   0-7445-5970-7

- *Captain Abdul's Pirate School* Colin McNaughton 0-7445-5242-7

- *The Ghost in Annie's Room* Philippa Pearce   0-7445-5993-6

- *Molly and the Beanstalk* Pippa Goodhart   0-7445-5981-2

- *Taking the Cat's Way Home* Jan Mark   0-7445-8268-7

- *The Finger-eater* Dick King-Smith   0-7445-8269-5

- *Care of Henry* Anne Fine   0-7445-8270-9

- *The Haunting of Pip Parker* Anne Fine   0-7445-8294-6

- *Cup Final Kid* Martin Waddell   0-7445-8297-0

- *Lady Long-legs* Jan Mark   0-7445-8296-2

- *Ronnie and the Giant Millipede* Jenny Nimmo   0-7445-8298-9

- *Emmelina and the Monster* June Crebbin   0-7445-8904-5

- *Posh Watson* Gillian Cross   0-7445-8271-7

- *Impossible Parents* Brian Patten   0-7445-9022-1

- *Holly and the Skyboard* Ian Whybrow   0-7445-9021-3

- *Patrick's Perfect Pet* Annalena McAfee   0-7445-8911-8

- *Me and My Big Mouse* Simon Cheshire   0-7445-5982-0

- *No Tights for George!* June Crebbin   0-7445-5999-5

All at £3.99